Lincoln School Library
La Porte, Indiana

DISCARDED

W9-BSM-218

LEO, ZACK, AND EMMIE

LEO, ZACK, AND EMMIE

by Amy Ehrlich
pictures by Steven Kellogg

THE DIAL PRESS · NEW YORK

Published by
The Dial Press
1 Dag Hammarskjold Plaza
New York, New York 10017

Text copyright © 1981 by Amy Ehrlich
Pictures copyright © 1981 by Steven Kellogg
All rights reserved. Manufactured in the U.S.A.
First Printing

Library of Congress Cataloging in Publication Data
Ehrlich, Amy, 1942– Leo, Zack, and Emmie.
Summary: The new girl in Zack and Leo's class
affects the boys' friendship.
[1. Friendship—Fiction]   I. Kellogg, Steven.
II. Title.
PZ7.E328Le   [E]   81-2604
ISBN 0-8037-4761-6 (lib. bdg.)   AACR2
ISBN 0-8037-4760-8 (pbk.)

The art for each picture consists of a black line-drawing
and three halftone separations.

Reading Level 2.2

CONTENTS

A NEW GIRL

There was a new girl
in Zack and Leo's class.
"Class," said Miss Davis,
"this is Emmie Williams.
Please make her feel welcome
in Room 208."

Miss Davis turned to write
some numbers on the blackboard.
Emmie Williams stuck out her tongue
and wiggled her ears.

No one saw but Zack.

He had tried to wiggle

his ears for years.

11

"Want to come over to my house?"
Leo said to Zack after school.
"I have a brand-new robot."
But Zack was waiting for Emmie.

"Maybe I'll come later,"
he said.

Emmie came into the schoolyard.

"Hi," said Zack.

"I know how to cross my eyes."

"Big deal," said Emmie.

She crossed her eyes

and looked straight at him.

Then she wiggled her ears.

"See you," she said and

walked away.

Zack went to Leo's house.

He went into the bathroom
and closed the door.

Then he looked in the mirror.

He held his ears with his fingers.

He moved them up and down.

It was no use.

When he took his fingers away,

his ears stayed right where

they were.

"Come on out of the bathroom,"
yelled Leo.

"Don't you want to see my robot?"

Leo's new robot
could walk and talk.
It could even shoot missiles.
But Zack did not want
to play with it.

"That Emmie Williams thinks

she's so great," he said.

"But I don't like her at all."

Leo shot a missile at the ceiling.

"I think she's nice," he said.

"Did you see how fast she ran

at playtime?

And she knows the names

of all the dinosaurs."

Zack did not want to hear about it.

"I'll show her," he said.

"Emmie Williams thinks

wiggling her ears

is the best thing

anyone could ever do."

"Well, that's not so much," said Leo.

He put the robot carefully in its box.

He took off his baseball cap.

Then he wiggled his ears up and down
about twenty times.

"Leo!" Zack yelled.

"You never told me
you could wiggle your ears."

"You never asked me," said Leo.

"It's easy.

I'll show you how."

Zack and Leo practiced

until Zack got it right.

Then they wiggled their ears

at each other

for the rest of the afternoon.

PLAYTIME

It was playtime.

Everyone had a partner

as they walked through the halls

to the schoolyard.

Zack and Leo held hands.

They were always partners

at playtime.

Zack brought out his ball.

It was big and soft,

because it was made out of sponge.

They tried to play catch,

but Leo kept missing the ball.

It sailed past his arms.

It rolled under his legs.

It hit him gently in the nose.

"Leo," said Zack,

"you're a good friend

but as a ballplayer, you stink.

I think I would rather play alone."

He threw the ball at the wall,

and it came back.

Back and forth. Over and over.

He caught it every time.

Suddenly a person

as fast as a streak

grabbed the ball on a bounce.

It was Emmie Williams.

"Who asked you into this game?"

said Zack.

Emmie did not answer.

She took off running
with the ball held close
like a football player.
Zack was getting mad.

"Hey, where are you going
with my ball?" he yelled.

Emmie slid down the slide
before Zack could climb the ladder.

She ran along the seesaw

faster than a tightrope walker.

Then she swung on the swings.

But when she headed for the jungle gym,
Zack was ready for her.
Whap! He grabbed her legs,
and she fell over.
The ball tumbled away in the sand
under the jungle gym.

As they rushed to get it
their heads knocked together hard.
"Ouch!" said Zack.
"That hurt!" said Emmie.

They looked at each other.

They were covered with sand.

They were on their hands and knees.

There was not even room to fight.

Emmie gave Zack his ball,
and they climbed to the top
of the jungle gym.

The schoolyard was empty.
Playtime was over.

"Race you to the school door,"
Emmie said.

They ran as fast as they could,
but it was a tie.

Inside the building
Zack took Emmie's hand.
They were partners
as they walked through the halls
back to Room 208.

HALLOWEEN

It was one week before Halloween.

Zack was going to be Batman.

Emmie was going to be a witch.

But Leo would not say

what his costume was.

"Please tell us," said Zack.

"Is it a superhero?" asked Emmie.

"No," said Leo,

"it's a surprise."

All week long Emmie and Zack

worked on their costumes.

One day they went

to the five-and-ten to buy masks.

Leo was in the checkout line.

He was buying glitter
and silver paper,
but he still wouldn't say
what his costume was.

Finally Zack knew what to do.

He went to Leo's house

and rang the bell.

"Hi, Leo," he said.

"Want to come trick-or-treating

with Emmie and me

on Halloween night?"

"Sure," said Leo.

"There's just one thing," said Zack.

"Only people who tell

what they are wearing can come."

Leo thought it over.

"Okay," he said at last.

"I'm going to be a snowflake."

"A snowflake!" shouted Zack.

"That's really dumb!

That's the dumbest costume

I ever heard of!"

Leo just smiled.

"Oh, well," he said.

"I guess I'll go alone."

On Halloween night
a full moon shone brightly.
Zack and Emmie saw superheroes
walking with pirates,
mummies walking with robots,
and gypsies walking with ghosts.

41

Zack saw three other Batmen.

Emmie counted six other witches.

But they did not say anything
about it to each other.

Suddenly a bright starry shape
came toward them.

As it came closer

Zack and Emmie could see colors

flashing like a million jewels.

"Ooooh, how beautiful!" said Emmie.

Then they both gasped.

It was Leo in his snowflake costume.

They all got to the next house
at the same time.
A lady came to the door.
"What a terrific snowflake!"
she said.
"And what's this?
Another Batman and another witch?"
She gave them all some candy
but she gave Leo more.

At every house

the same thing happened.

"Look," Zack whispered to Emmie,

"his trick-or-treat bag

is twice as full as ours."

As they walked along
everyone stopped Leo
to ask about his costume.
People even crossed the street
to look at it.

At last they got to Emmie's house.

As soon as they were inside

Zack took off his Batman cape.

"Hey, Leo, can I try on

your snowflake costume?" he asked.

"You mean this dumb thing?" said Leo.

"NO WAY!"

SHOW AND TELL

Everyone in Room 208

was sitting in a circle.

They were having Show and Tell.

Leo and Emmie had both

brought in plants to show.

Emmie had a potato vine

and Leo had a cactus.

"Class," said Miss Davis,
"these plants look very different,
but many things about them
are the same.

I would like Emmie and Leo
to do a report about plants
for Monday."

"I want to work on the report too,"
Zack said at lunch.

"But, Zack," said Emmie,
"Miss Davis told only
Leo and me to do it."
Zack picked up his lunch box
and moved to another table.

The rest of the week

he would not talk to them.

"He's feeling bad about our report,"

said Leo.

"If you ask me,

he's acting like a dope," said Emmie.

On Monday Leo and Emmie were ready.

At Show and Tell

they showed Room 208

a model of a giant plant.

They told how the roots,

the leaves, and the flowers

helped the plant to grow.

Then they sang a song about plants:

"Oh, the roots are connected

to the stem.

And the stem is connected
to the leaves.
And the leaves are connected
to the flowers.
And the flowers are connected
to the seeds."
Everyone joined the singing.
Everyone but Zack.
He looked like he was going to cry.

After school Emmie and Leo decided
to try to talk to him.
Emmie carried the model of
the giant plant.
Leo took a lunch box in each hand.
When they got to Zack's house,
they could not find him at first.

Then they saw him.

He was sitting in a tree.

He would not come down,

so Leo and Emmie climbed up.

"Don't talk to me," Zack said.

"I don't want you to talk to me."

They sat there quietly

in the tree.

A wind came up and blew the leaves off the branches.

It began to get dark.

At last Zack started to say what was wrong.

"Leo was my friend
before he was your friend,"
he told Emmie.

"And he wouldn't even know you
if it wasn't for me.

But ever since you two began

working on your plant report,

you're always together

and you don't like me anymore."

"Why do you think

we're up here then?" asked Emmie.

"Yes, why do you think

we came over?" asked Leo.

"Za—ack, where aaare you?"

It was Zack's mother calling.

"I'm getting cold," said Leo.

"I'm getting tired of this tree,"
said Zack.

"Come on. Let's go."

He climbed down,
and Leo and Emmie followed.
The model of the giant plant
was lying in the grass.
Zack picked it up.

"Hey, this thing's pretty neat.

Was it hard to make?" he asked.

"No," said Emmie, "it was easy.

We'll show you how."